Prairie Chicken Little

Published by
PEACHTREE PUBLISHERS
1700 Chattahoochee Avenue
Atlanta, Georgia 30318-2112
www.peachtree-online.com

Text © 2013 by Jackie Mims Hopkins
Illustrations © 2013 by Henry Cole

First trade paperback edition published in 2015

Design and composition by Loraine M. Joyner

The illustrations were created in watercolor, ink, and colored pencil on 100% rag, archival watercolor paper. Title typeset in Adobe System Inc.'s Nueva by Carol Twombly; text typeset in Microsoft Corporation's Tahoma by Matthew Carter.

Printed in November 2018 by RR Donnelley & Sons in China
10 9 8 7 6 5 4 3 (hardcover)
10 9 8 7 6 5 4 (trade paperback)

HC ISBN: 978-1-56145-694-9
PB ISBN: 978-1-56145-834-9

Library of Congress Cataloging-in-Publication Data

Hopkins, Jackie.
Prairie chicken little / written by Jackie Mims Hopkins; illustrated by Henry Cole.
p. cm.
ISBN 978-1-56145-694-9
Summary: In this retelling of the classic tale, Mary McBlicken, a small prairie chicken, and her animal friends are on their way to tell Cowboy Stan and Red Dog Dan that a stampede is coming when they meet a hungry coyote.
[1. Folklore.] I. Cole, Henry, 1955— ill. II. Chicken Licken. III. Title.
PZ8.1.H854Pr 2013
398.2—dc23
[E]
2012025540

For Addison, my sweet little chickadee, and her daddy, Jonathan,
and thanks to Bill and Susan Garrison for their Red Dog Dan inspiration
—*J. M. H.*

To my favorite prairie chicken, Joan, with love, Hen
—*H. C.*

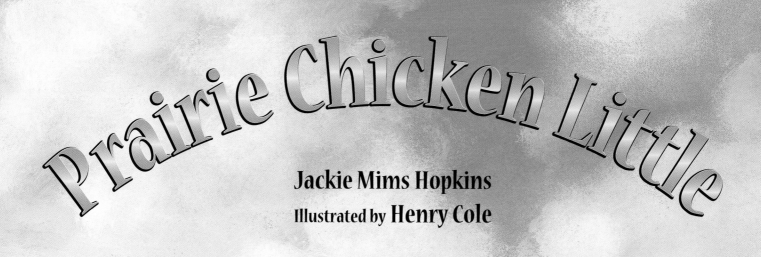

Prairie Chicken Little

Jackie Mims Hopkins

Illustrated by Henry Cole

PEACHTREE
ATLANTA

Out on the grasslands where bison roam, Mary McBlicken the prairie chicken was scritch-scratching for her breakfast, when all of a sudden she heard a rumbling and a grumbling and a tumbling.

"Oh no!" she exclaimed. "A stampede's a comin'! I need to hightail it back to the ranch to tell Cowboy Stan and Red Dog Dan. They'll know what to do."

So away Mary ran, lickety-splickety, as fast as her little prairie chicken legs could carry her.

On her way to the ranch, Mary came upon Jeffrey Snog the prairie dog, who was soaking up some sunshine.

"Good mornin' to you," barked Jeffrey.

"No time for good mornin's," warned Mary. "A stampede's a comin'!"

"How do you know that this is so?" asked Jeffrey.

"I heard a rumblin' and a grumblin' and a tumblin'—I did!" said Mary.

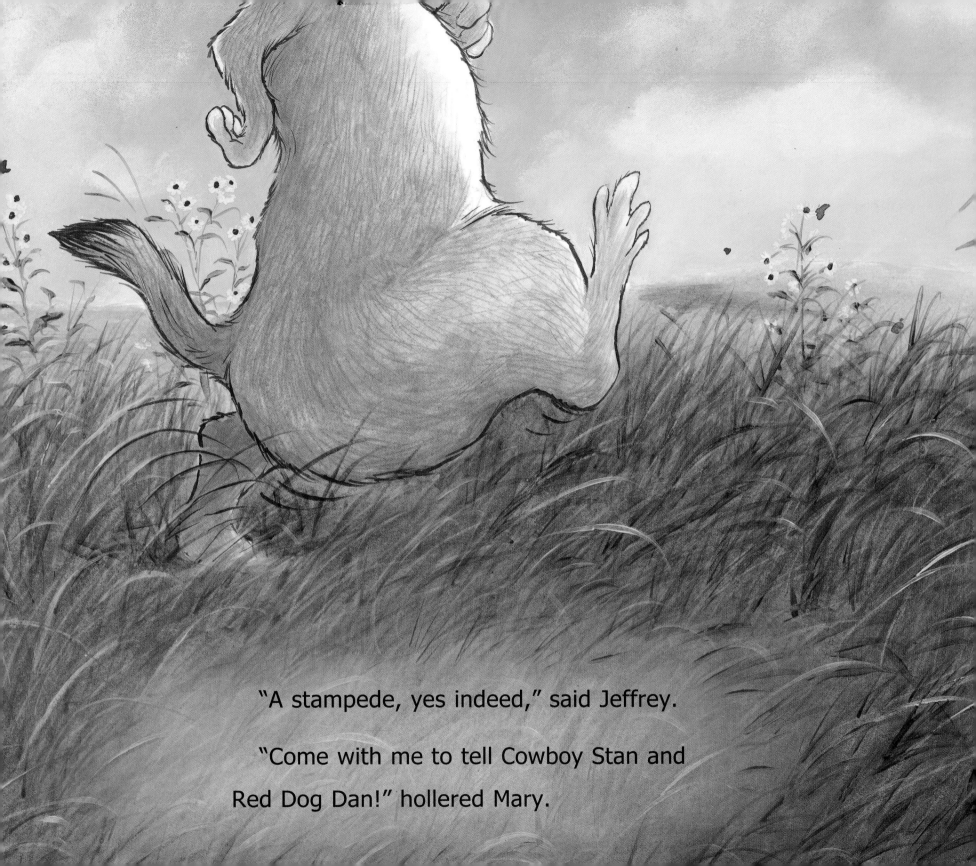

"A stampede, yes indeed," said Jeffrey.

"Come with me to tell Cowboy Stan and
Red Dog Dan!" hollered Mary.

"Let's hit the trail!" barked Jeffrey. And away the pair ran, lickety-splickety, toward the ranch.

Soon they met Beau Grabbit the jack rabbit, who was nibbling on some sweet grass.

"Where are you two going in such a hurry?" he asked.

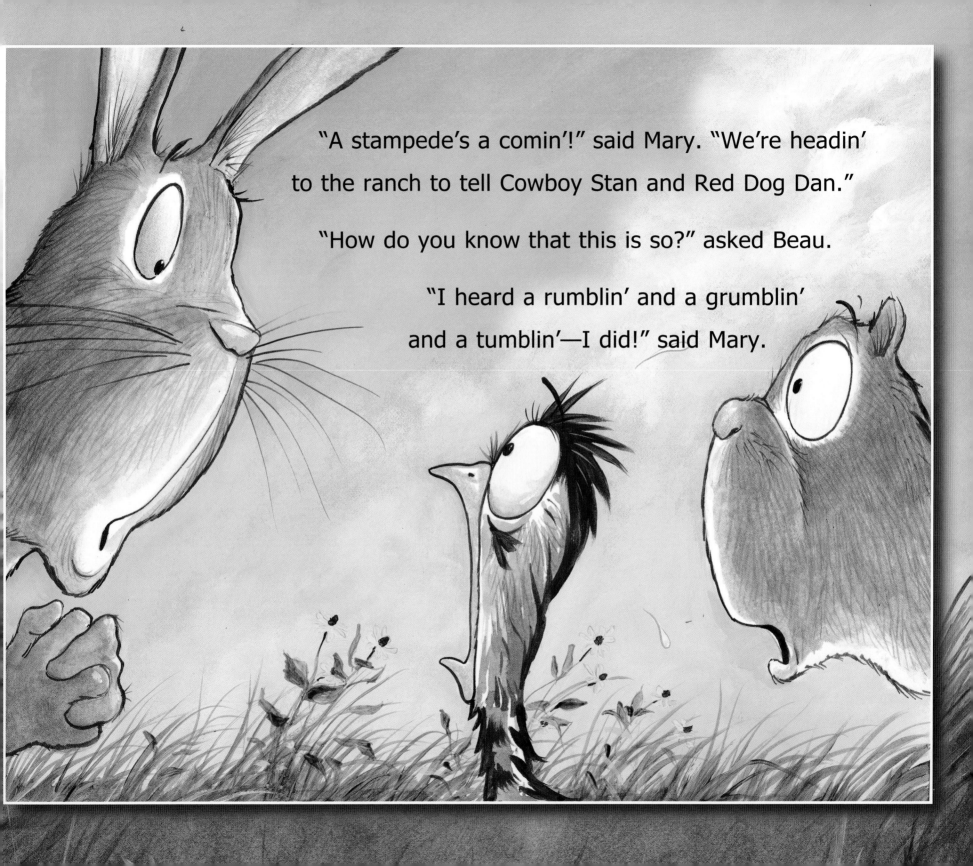

"A stampede's a comin'!" said Mary. "We're headin'
to the ranch to tell Cowboy Stan and Red Dog Dan."

"How do you know that this is so?" asked Beau.

"I heard a rumblin' and a grumblin'
and a tumblin'—I did!" said Mary.

"A stampede, yes indeed," said Beau.

"Come with us to tell Cowboy Stan
and Red Dog Dan!" hollered Mary.

"Let's hop to it then," said Beau.

And they lit off across the prairie, lickety-splickety, toward the ranch.

Before long, the trio came across
June Spark the meadowlark, who was
building her nest in the tall prairie grass.

"What's going on?" asked June.

"A stampede's a comin'!" chorused the trio.

"How do you know that this is so?" asked June.

"I heard a rumblin' and a grumblin'
and a tumblin'—I did!" said Mary.

"A stampede, yes indeed,"
said June.

"Come with us to tell Cowboy Stan and Red Dog Dan!" hollered Mary.

"What are we waitin' for?" chirped June.

And away they all flew, lickety-splickety, toward the ranch.

It wasn't long before Slim Brody the sly coyote spotted them making their way across the prairie.

"Well, hello there, my fine feathered and furry friends. What's the big rush?"

"A stampede's a comin'! We're headin' to the ranch to tell Cowboy Stan and Red Dog Dan," said Mary.

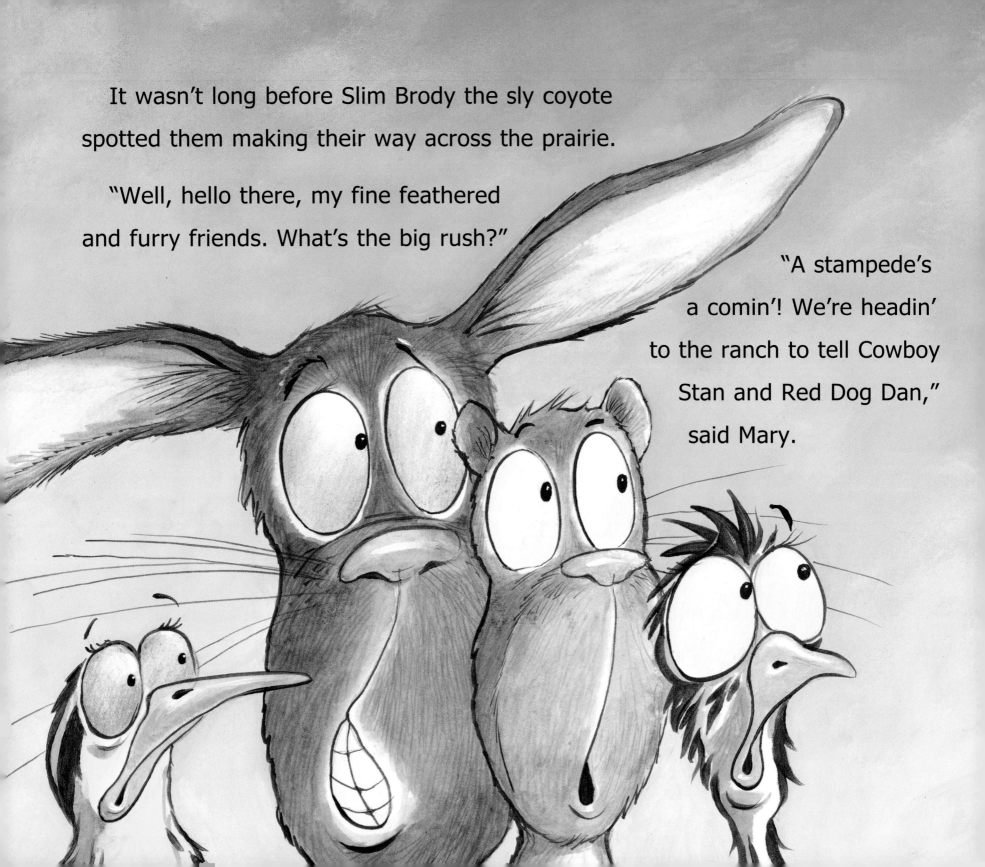

"It's your lucky day," said Slim.

"I just happen to know a shortcut."

He had no intention of taking them to the ranch.

Instead, he led them across the plain,

over a hill,

through a pass,

around a bend,

and down a gully

to the entrance of his den.

"What's this?"
squawked Mary.

"This," snarled Slim, "is the passage to the shortcut." He flashed a toothy smile and closed in on Mary McBlicken and the others.

The fine feathered and furry friends all
started clucking and barking and thumping
and chirping as loud as they could.

Cowboy Stan and Red Dog Dan heard the ruckus and came charging across the prairie toward the den. Dan made a beeline for Slim Brody and chased that coyote, lickety-splickety, far, far, away.

"What's going on?" asked Stan.

"A stampede's a comin'!" cried Mary.

"How do you know that this is so?" asked Stan.

But before Mary could open her beak to speak, everyone heard a rumbling and a grumbling and a tumbling—yes indeed!

"Why, that's not a stampede," said Stan, "that's your stomach! There's only one way to head off a rumbling and a grumbling and a tumbling stomach.

"You need some grub!"

So, Cowboy Stan cooked up a fine supper for those critters and that took care of Mary McBlicken's stomach stampede, lickety-splickety, yes indeed.